THE ISLAND MURDER
A Novella

SINCLAIR MACLEOD

MARPLESI
BOOKS

Published in 2013 by Marplesi

ISBN Paperback: 978-0-9931307-5-5
Ebook: 978-0-9575566-0-7

A catalogue record for this book is available
from the British Library.

Dedication

To Iain and Margaret
for shared memories of happy days

As always, in memory of Calum,
my wonderful son and constant guiding light.

Acknowledgements

As always my love and thanks also go to my wife of 25 years, Kim and my incredibly wise and gorgeous daughter, Kirsten. I could not write these books without their continued love, support and inspiration.

CHAPTER 1

The small ferry tossed, pitched and tossed again. It caused my stomach to roil, heave and roil in time with the unpredictable motion and I was struggling to keep the contents intact. Thankfully, the journey to the island of Little Cumbrae was only fifteen minutes long and it was with some relief that I boarded my bike, rolled it off the disembarkation ramp and onto the island.

The excursion had originally been planned as a boys' weekend for Li and I. Our lives were so hectic we rarely got time to have a beer and talk. Carol was away on a hen weekend with some of her friends and I thought that it would be the perfect time for my mate and I to catch up. Li had suggested we visit Millport as he had heard a lot about it but had never been there and the kid in him loved the idea of getting on a bike to cycle round the island in between nights of drinking, snacking and chatting.

His business was growing quickly and he had added another high-class barbershop to the original in Garnethill. He hadn't taken even a weekend break for over eighteen months and was looking forward to our trip but he called late on Friday to say that he had contracted some stomach virus and wouldn't be able to make it.

I had called and cancelled his room at the guesthouse but decided that a nostalgic trip back to a place where I had spent many a happy short holiday was just what I needed to give me a boost.

The island is off the coast of west Ayrshire and is only three miles long and ten miles around. There is one town, Millport, and the total population is around fifteen hundred people. It has its own historic castle - one that played a role in the English Civil War - and the smallest cathedral in the United Kingdom.

When I was a kid, it was a place to spend a 'Fair Holiday' weekend or an Easter Monday. It was a safe haven where you could join the host of other families who went there to enjoy eating ice cream and cycling around its outer road.

I rolled my own motorised bike onto that very road and began the journey from the ferry point to the town itself. The wind had been picking up all day and the cotton clouds raced across a cerulean sky as if they had somewhere better to be. Seagulls battled against the wind and then changed direction to be swept away in the opposite direction as if that was the way they had always intended to go. There were warnings of an autumnal storm hitting the west coast of Scotland within the next twenty-four hours and I began to wonder if my break was ill-fated.

The island road was suffering from neglect and in places was pot holed and uneven which made me concentrate for much of the way. On one side the dark blue sea was capped with white breaking waves while on the shore side the bracken and ferns on the hillside had garbed themselves in their winter colours of russet brown and straw yellow. Further up the hill the trees were casting off their leaves as they retreated in the face of the approaching North European winter.

Despite the buffeting of the wind, I enjoyed slaloming the bike around the curves, remembering fondly mellow summer days with my mother and father by my side as we pedalled to a picnic.

When I reached the hard right turn that would take me into the haven of Millport Bay, those warm feelings became even stronger. The town hadn't changed much in the twenty years since I had last visited; the same mixture of sandstone and pastel-painted buildings lined the seafront, protecting the narrow streets behind them and projecting respectable solidity. It gave the impression of a place that has cut itself off from the rest of the world, a bit like Brigadoon without the fog. I rode past the guesthouses, private homes, holiday flats and shops that were a world away from the package hotels, holiday villas and sunshine beaches that were now the regular destination for the majority of Glaswegian holidaymakers. Millport's time as a bustling summer town was long gone but it held on to a genteel dignity that offered relaxation and simple pleasures.

I found my way to the guesthouse in Howard Street, tucked away from the exposed seafront. I parked the bike, removed my backpack and walked up to the ice-blue door of a white house.

An attractive middle-aged woman opened the door before I could knock. She was dressed in a stylish array of clothes, all in seasonal tones that matched the bracken and trees. Her hair was dyed a startling auburn and her green eyes twinkled with youthful mischief.

"Mr Campbell?"

"That's me," I replied and smiled.

"I'm Eileen Jackson. Come away in and I'll take you to your room."

I followed her into a narrow hall and onto an even narrower stairway that was covered with a thick, patterned carpet. We walked up two flights of steep steps before reaching my room.

"Is this your first time in Millport?" she asked as she unlocked the attic room door.

"No, I used to be a regular when I was a youngster."

"Aye, a lot of people used to be regulars, not so much these days." It was a fleeting regret but she held on to her good humour.

The door swung open onto a compact room where the eaves of the roof sloped so low that I wasn't able to stand upright at the sides - I thought that I would have to be careful that I didn't bang my head in the middle of the night. There was a single bed, a bedside cabinet with a lamp and a wardrobe. A door at the opposite end of the room led to a small toilet and shower room. It was clean, smelled pleasantly of pine and was an ideal place to spend a weekend.

"Your pal couldn't make it?" she asked.

"No, he caught some kind of bug. I thought I would come anyway just to recharge the batteries."

"What is it you do?"

"I'm an insurance investigator," I replied. I didn't think the poor woman would want to hear about some of the grisly tales of kidnap and murder that I had been involved in since my involuntary change of career. I always chose carefully the time and place to introduce the subject of private investigations.

"Oh, that must be interesting," she said politely while her expression showed that she thought it really wasn't and she was probably stifling a yawn.

"Breakfast is from seven until nine and I'd be grateful if you could pay me once you've got yourself settled and before you go out."

"I will do, thanks."

"If you're fond of a wee puff of hash or anything else, please not in the room but the garden's secluded, no one would see you." She winked. There was something in her manner that suggested if I needed some special form of relaxation, she would be able to source it.

"No worries on that score, Eileen."

She laughed in a wicked way and left. There was more to Mrs Eileen Jackson than met the eye.

I spent the next hour unpacking and then levering myself into the tiny shower that wasn't much wider than my shoulders. It was a test of ingenuity to complete the washing process but when it was over I dressed in jeans, T-shirt and a warm jumper. I decided to take a quick walk around town before grabbing a bite to eat.

I walked back down the precarious stairway and found Eileen in the kitchen. I paid her what I owed for my stay and then headed out into the great metropolis.

When I turned on to the promenade, I felt the full force of the ever-strengthening wind. I pulled the zip of my jacket up around my neck and huddled down into its warmth.

I strolled along the small row of shops; a mixture of cafés and gift shops for the tourists, butchers and grocers for the locals. The bicycle hire shops were closed; the opening hours were much shorter in the chill of October than they were on a balmy July day. There weren't too many people around and it was a pleasant, if chilly stroll.

I crossed the broad road to the shore side exposing me to the salty spray that was being skimmed off the water by the force of the wind. I walked briskly along towards the Crocodile Rock, Millport's unique feature. The rock looks vaguely crocodilian in shape but the similarity is emphasised by the lurid eyes and sharp teeth that have been painted on it. That day it was being battered by the waves as the gale pounded them on to the shoreline as if they were trying to erode Millport's big tourist attraction into something less fierce. I continued to walk until I was almost at the edge of the town and then turned to head back when I heard the distinctive roar of motorcycle engines. I watched as a line of around twelve bikes rounded the point and rode into town. It was like a scene from the 'Wild One' and as a fan I was delighted to see that every rider was sitting on a Ducati. I saluted them as they rode passed me and then followed their path back to the heart of the town.

The bikes were lined up in a row outside one of the cafés on the front. I cast envious eyes along the array of stylish Italian machines. The oldest was a 750 GT from the early seventies, its tank was painted in a shade of red that was more muted than the lurid scarlet you would find on a modern bike. Other highlights of the collection included a late eighties 906 in canary yellow and a ST4S grand tourer. It was the same model I had owned before it had been destroyed in a fire while I worked on the search for a missing woman and there were times when I missed its nimble handling.

I decided I had to meet this group of like-minded apostles, so I walked into the café where the members of the 'gang' were the only customers. There were ten men and two women, all dressed in heavy bike leathers; to one side their helmets were arranged on a table like a tray of painted Easter eggs.

I asked for a coffee and a sandwich. When my order arrived I decided to learn more about these fellow travellers.

"Hi, that's a cracking collection of bikes."

"Hello, they are indeed. Are you into bikes yourself?" a man with a bushy grey beard and a jovial grin asked.

"I am, a Ducati man, in fact I have a 1200s. It's the second one I've owned, I had a ST4S before that."

"That's mine out there," a small man said in a surprisingly deep voice.

"It's a good machine, unfortunately I lost mine in an accident." Once again I avoided discussing some of the details of my role as a private detective. The bike had been destroyed by fire after a disturbed man had shot a couple of bullets into it.

"Why don't you join us?" the happy beard said.

"I would be delighted. I'm Craig, Craig Campbell," I said as I swung a chair around from another table and joined them at the three Formica-topped tables that they had grouped together.

"I'm Neil Cairns and we're the committee of the Ducati Owners of Scozia club; the Ducateers to our friends. I'm the chairperson and most folk just call me Rev," he said with a bonhomie that was infectious.

"Rev?"

He stood up and turned to show me the back of his leather jacket. Across the shoulders were stitched the words 'God's Biker" and below them was a motorcycle helmet topped with a halo.

"I'm a retired Church Of Scotland minister. I've always loved motorbikes ever since I was a kid and I thought why should it only be the angels from Hell that have all the fun," he laughed and I joined him politely.

"This is our treasurer, Deborah Grayson." He indicated a stunning blonde-haired woman who I guessed was in her mid-thirties. Her face glowed with natural beauty; her dark blue eyes, elegant cheek bones, petite nose and full lips gave her a Nordic look that would leave most straight men buckling at the knees.

"Hi," she said brightly. The way she held herself and smiled indicated she knew exactly what kind of effect she had on the opposite sex.

Next was the secretary, Colin Victor, who was the owner of the ST4S and the deep voice.

Next to Ms Grayson, the other woman looked plain. She had short brown hair, a pale complexion and sad brown eyes. Her name was Rhona McColl and she muttered an almost inaudible greeting.

The rest of the men were introduced and I quickly forgot their names with the exception of the youngest in the group. He was called Brent Picard and looked every inch the guy that would have been bullied all the way through school. He was in his mid-twenties with lank, greasy red hair that hung from a bandana decorated with the stars and stripes. Under his jacket I could see a T-shirt that read 'Bikers do it flat out'.

His complexion was pasty white with areas of fiery red acne. His glasses were a couple generations out of date; the thick lenses magnified his muddy brown eyes.

"Hi, dude," he said when he was introduced.

Inwardly, I groaned; I wondered why no one had taken him aside and tried to get him to turn down the geek meter.

"So, what does an owners club do?" I asked Rev.

"Well, quite a lot. We get together to exchange knowledge about the bikes; we go on weekend rides; we organise track days for the more adventurous among us and we raise money for spinal injury charities. We've got a website where you can buy and sell bikes and parts. Oh and most importantly we have a bit of a laugh."

"Sounds good." I said.

"You should join, we're always looking for new blood," Deborah said with another flirtatious tilt of her head.

"I might just do that. So what brings you to Millport in the teeth of an autumn gale?"

"We have a committee outing a couple of times a year, to plan the events for the next session and decide on the charity we're going to support. We could do it in Glasgow but it's become a bit of a tradition to come here," the Rev. replied.

"We're having a bit of a dinner and drink later, you should join us," Rhona said.

"That's very kind, where and when?"

She gave me the name of the pub and told me to be there at seven-thirty. We spent half an hour talking about motorbikes before they said they had to go. They were staying in some self-catering flats on the other side of the town from where I was based and we went our separate ways at the café door.

I walked back to my own temporary home and I was glad of the heat of the room when I arrived. I was looking forward to a more sociable evening than I had anticipated.

CHAPTER 2

I spent the rest of the afternoon lying on the bed reading a science fiction novel by Iain M. Banks. I rarely took time to read, other than when I was on holiday but my unplanned solitude offered an ideal opportunity. Mrs Jackson appeared at one point to make sure I had settled in and that the room was comfortable enough for me. I assured her that everything was fine but before she left, she once again hinted that if I were looking for something exotic to smoke, she would be able to supply it. I thanked her but refused her kind - if illegal - offer.

Around seven I laid the book aside and got dressed. I had packed a royal blue shirt, dark blue formal trousers and a pair of black brogues. Before I met Carol, Li used to joke that he always knew when I was on the pull because I wasn't working and yet I was wearing something other than a T-shirt, jeans and trainers. I wasn't looking for female company, but I thought that I should make an effort, as the committee members had been kind enough to invite me to share their evening.

When I walked out of the guesthouse, the clear skies had been blown away and been replaced by heavy rainclouds that were releasing steadily their contents on the town. I hurried through the storm to the pub and was relieved to be back in the warmth and light.

I was expecting a traditional Scottish pub but instead the interior was filled with light-coloured wood, modern lighting and designer flourishes. There was a horseshoe-shaped bar, which had a well-stocked gantry and an array of beers. Directly opposite the end of the bar was a roaring wood fire that was both a welcoming and welcome sight.

The committee members were already seated around a long table that looked like it had been made from polished driftwood; full of knots, swirls and irregular shapes. A seat had been left for me between the Reverend Cairns and Deborah Grayson. She patted the chair and said, "You're beside me, Craig."

I accepted the invitation but I was already on my guard. Ms. Grayson appeared to have me firmly in her sights.

The meal was excellent, more restaurant standard than I had expected from a local pub. There was a steady supply of wine served to the table but I restricted myself to a couple of glasses. The majority of the others weren't so hesitant and by the time the tea and coffee were served, some members of the party were showing the effects.

When the meal was finished, the pub was beginning to fill with regulars and the barman asked us if we could move to allow a band some space to set up. We moved around to a small set of tables at the other side of the bar, while some members of the bikers group stood at the bar.

The band was a small folk trio comprising of a guitar, fiddle and accordion. They played a variety of Scottish, Irish and American music with an adeptness that helped to boost the pub's comfortable, hospitable Scottish ambience.

Within ten minutes of the move I found myself cornered by the exotically named Brent. Apart from ditching the bandana, he was still sporting the same clothes he had been wearing that afternoon. There was a slightly bitter smell of sweat emanating from him, which I had to endure more potently as the bar became crowded and I was pressed closer to him by the crush of people.

"Brent Picard isn't my real name," he told me after we had been talking for about ten minutes.

"Really?" I replied in fake surprise.

"No, I used to be Shane Brown but that was totally boring, man. I decided to change it by deed poll. I thought Jean-Luc was a bit much and Data Picard didn't sound right, so I used the actor's name instead. You know, Brent Spiner?"

I nodded. In an effort to steer the conversation away from his Star Trek obsession, I asked, "What do you do for a living?"

"I'm an I.T. guy. Servers in fact."

I should have guessed, I thought.

"I look after Windows 2008 servers for a company in Cambuslang. I have twenty-five on a full virtual server rack with ten terabytes of storage space. I'm just designing a plan to upgrade to 2012…"

I found myself tuning out as he spun off into computer heaven and prattled on about network capacity, virtual PCs and the joys of creating your own home network.

He was in the middle of a rambling tale of how he and his mates had created their own guild in some online role playing game when Deborah Grayson pushed her way through the crowd.

"Craig, there you are. Let me rescue you from this boring little man."

Before I could reply she continued, "Do you know he once had the audacity to ask me out on a date? Hah! Imagine him thinking he had a chance with me. Come with me and we'll talk about something more interesting."

She grabbed my arm and pulled me through the crowd to a table. I mouthed 'sorry' to Brent/Shane who looked both embarrassed and furious at Deborah's rude interruption. I couldn't blame him and felt a little sorry for him as he was left nursing his pint and a lot of resentment.

I was annoyed at Grayson's behaviour and told her so. "That was extremely rude."

She waved her hand in a dismissive gesture and said, "Oh, don't worry about him, he's a pathetic child. Rides a motorbike to try to make him more interesting. And that name, Brent Picard, what a joke."

She seemed to think that her fellow biker wasn't worthy of her consideration or even simple human decency.

She levered a space for the two of us between the Reverend Cairns and Rhona McColl. Both parties looked put out but once again Ms. Grayson was completely oblivious.

She was dressed in a carnation pink satin blouse - with the top buttons undone to show the top of her breasts - tight black jeans and black stiletto heels. Everything she wore, including her jewellery and perfume only added to her natural allure. Despite the window dressing, I found nothing attractive about her as her character fell far short of her looks.

I spent the next half an hour at the mercy of every flirting technique she had in her armoury. I fended her off with platitudes, frequent references to the relationship I enjoyed with Carol and a sense of polite detachment. When the fluttering eyes, flashes of cleavage and little touches of my thigh didn't work, she began to lose interest. I could see Rhona's smile growing wider as Deborah became more and more frustrated at my lack of interest.

I offered to buy a round and escaped the blonde woman's clutches by going to the bar.

As he was serving me, the barman said in a broad Lancashire accent, "You in the Ducati club?"

"No, I met them this afternoon. I own a bike myself, so I started talking to them and they invited me to join them. As I was on my own, I thought why not."

"She's quite a woman, that Deborah."

I replied neutrally, "Eh… yes, do you know her well? I'm Craig Campbell by the way."

"Nathan Grimshaw. She's a regular visitor to the island. She likes a bit of fun." I couldn't quite read it but there was a definite undercurrent to his statement. He turned away to get some more drinks and Rhona McColl appeared at my side.

"I thought I'd give you a hand."

"Thanks."

"I see you're managing to avoid the claws of the blonde vixen," she said with a grin.

"Just about."

"She's had more men than the Highland Light Infantry and will always move on to another challenge once her conquest is complete."

"What do you mean?"

"There aren't many men who are capable of defeating her plans for domination. If you catch my meaning." There was a spiteful element to what she was saying and it could be that she was simply jealous but having seen Deborah in action I could understand where she was coming from. I had felt the power of Deborah's obvious sexuality being used as a weapon to weaken my defences.

"I prefer my women to be a little less…" I searched for the right word that wouldn't sound too insulting. "Obvious."

"She was in hospital a couple of months back for a procedure, if you know what I mean. Her loose morals caught up with her, I think," she said with a malevolent wink and a smile.

Before I could respond, she continued, "Did she tell you that she used to have a thing with the Neil?"

"Really?"

"She was the reason he left the church. It was quite a scandal about four years back. He was married and I think she decided that was enough to make him a target. He fell in love with her, left his wife and was thrown out of his job; he didn't really retire. Within six months she left him for another victim." I could see that she was savouring every juicy detail of the gossip.

"She sounds very calculating but I wouldn't have thought that Neil was her type."

"You mean the image?"

"Yeah, he looks like a traditional biker."

"The beard, the hair and the rest all arrived after she walked out on him. Underneath all that, he is a handsome man by all accounts. She broke his heart and he was in therapy for six months, a lot of anger and depression issues apparently. He became a different person by the time he had completed the therapy." I could see part of her was enjoying the scandal of the story; it was also a chance to have a good bitch about Deborah Grayson and I wondered what her real rationale was for the nasty undercurrent to what she was saying.

"He seems happy enough now."

"He puts on a brave face, it's all part of a persona he has created."

"Did Rev. bring her into the owner's club?"

"Yes, he's always loved bikes. I think she's stuck around because the vast majority of our members are men. She's like a lioness in a herd of wildebeest."

"You don't seem to like her very much."

"She's an A-class cow, the kind of woman that gives the rest of our sex a bad name," she said with a deep-set bitterness.

The barman had finished pouring our drinks and I paid him. Before we walked back to the table, Rhona said, "Don't be fooled by the dizzy blonde act she pulls, she's as scheming as any politician and twice as duplicitous."

Before we left the bar I noticed my landlady, Eileen, at the other side of the room. I nodded a greeting and she returned it with a broad smile.

We carried the drinks back to the table. Deborah turned, "Rhona been giving you her chat. A bit like being chatted up by Quasimodo really isn't it?" She was smiling but there was no hint of either genuine humour or warmth.

"Shut up," Rhona replied with enough malice that I thought she might swing a punch at the other woman.

"Now ladies, play nice," Neil Cairns said, trying to ease the tension.

Grayson just laughed.

I distributed the drinks and the company fell into an uncomfortable silence.

Colin Victor was sitting at the same table but had contributed nothing to the conversation. He seemed to be a naturally shy man but his reticence was a little unusual in a social situation where he knew the people around him. I tried to engage him, "What is it you do when you're not riding a bike, Colin?"

He looked at me and appeared to be considering his answer. "I work in a supermarket now but up until ten months ago I ran my own company."

"Did you retire?"

"No, I was forced out of business by someone who then picked up my company for a song." He stared at Deborah Grayson as he said it but she was lost in her usual self-absorbed bubble.

"There are plenty of people taking advantage of the recession," I said sympathetically.

"Yes, there are sharks in every pool, and some of them have blonde hair," he said with a quiet, simmering ire.

I was beginning to regret my decision to be part of this fractious little group.

I drifted away to talk to some of the other members of the Ducateers committee and around ten-thirty I decided to call it a night.

I said goodbye to the bikers and stepped out into the full force of a fierce storm. I had only gone a couple of steps when

I heard my name. I turned to see Deborah Grayson huddled in the shelter of a shop doorway.

Her left arm held her right arm at the elbow, her right hand was close to her face and a cigarette flared softly as she took a draw.

"Hi Debbie, I'm off to the guesthouse," I said.

"Come here," she said as she indicated with her head for me to join and then blew a plume of blue smoke into the air above her.

There wasn't much space between us when I squeezed into the doorway.

"You don't like me much, do you?" she asked. Her eyes were glazed over and it was obvious she was very drunk.

"I hardly know you," I replied carefully.

"Not many people like me but do you know what? I don't give a damn."

"It's kind of a lonely way to go through life."

"I spent the early years of my adulthood being screwed by other people. I learned that it's better to be the one doing the screwing." She offered no further detail but the pain was something she carried with her.

"Did that include Neil? Did he deserve to be screwed?"

She looked intently at me, struggling to focus but keen to impress upon me the importance of what she was saying.

"He was different. It started as a game, just another conquest but then I fell in love with him. He was so sweet, gentle and kind; unlike any guy I had ever known. I wasn't used to being treated that way, especially by a man. Then I went back to behaving like I always did. I didn't know how to handle his devotion, I didn't trust it, and I didn't trust him."

Whether it was the drink or genuine regret, I wasn't sure but there was no doubt that at that moment she was thinking of what might have been.

"Is that why you continue to torment him?"

"I don't know. It's just instinctive now."

"You might find that more people would like you if you could bury that instinct."

"I know. I know. What about you? Could you like me for one night? I would give you a night you wouldn't forget," she whispered as she pressed against me.

"I think you should go sleep it off. Maybe tomorrow's the day to start anew."

She stretched up and tried to kiss me on the lips but I diverted her attentions to my cheek. As she was in the process of offering the kiss, one of the men from the Ducateers was walking passed. He mumbled a greeting and embarrassed, walked on.

I turned my attention to Debbie once again. "Go to your flat. I'll see you in the morning."

"Fuck off, you're just like all the rest," she shouted before she staggered away in the direction of her lodgings.

I shook my head and hurried away. Whatever the tragedy of her earlier life, she had no excuse for the distaste she showed for her fellow human beings.

Thunder rolled as I reached the guesthouse and I was glad to be climbing into my bed, far from the gales, the unpredictable Deborah Grayson and the tempestuous relationships of the committee. I tried to read some more of the novel but my eyes were closing and I wasn't taking in details of the story. I put the book down and was soon fast asleep.

CHAPTER 3

The following morning I awoke at eight and after a shower made my way to the small dining room on the ground floor of the guesthouse. Mrs Jackson looked tired but she served a fantastic and enormous breakfast. She didn't say much and her playfulness seemed to have been exhausted the previous day. By the end of the meal I was in need of some exercise to work off some of the calories.

If anything, the storm had increased in ferocity by the time I stepped out for my walk. On the shore front waves were pounding on to the promenade wall and throwing great plumes of water into the air like nature's own dancing fountains. I stayed on the opposite side of the road and walked the length of the town, working off the sausage, bacon et al, that Mrs Jackson had fed me.

On the way back, I noticed the bikes were once again sitting outside the same café where I had met the riders the previous day. They had agreed to meet there for breakfast and all were assembled with one notable exception. There was no sign of the blonde head of Deborah Grayson.

"Good morning, Craig," the Rev. said.

"Good morning, all. How are your heads?"

There were some murmurs about feeling rough but they seemed to have survived the evening's excesses with few casualties.

"Has Deborah succumbed to her hangover?'

"We've not seen her," Colin replied.

"We thought she would be here by now, I'll give her a ring." Brent picked up his phone and tapped it before lifting it to his ear. He seemed to be seeking desperately for approval from Neil and the rest of the group. He waited a few seconds but there was no reply. I could hear the faint sound of a voicemail system asking him to leave a message.

"No reply. That's a bit strange."

"Maybe we should check if she's OK," I suggested.

The guy who had passed Deborah and I when she had kissed me was the first to volunteer, "I'll go. She was in the same flat as me anyway."

"Sorry, what's your name?" I asked.

"Pat McKean."

"Cheers, Pat."

He looked at me strangely before he left.

"Would you like something to eat, Craig?" Rhona McColl asked.

"No, thanks. My landlady was more than generous with her portions at breakfast. I'm stuffed. I'll get a coffee."

I ordered a cappuccino and joined the group. One or two were looking a little rough around the edges and the conversation was a little stilted.

After ten minutes, Pat arrived back on the bike. He rushed into the café, removing his helmet as he walked. "She's not there. Her bed's not been slept in," he said hurriedly

"Probably found some poor bastard to keep her occupied all night," I heard Rhona say under her breath.

"I'll try her mobile again," Neil Cairns offered.

The same process brought the same result as Brent's attempt. Cairns had loved Deborah Grayson once and by his tone it was clear that his warm feelings for her hadn't evaporated entirely.

The investigator in me had the first little tickle of doubt. "Was her bike outside the flat?" I asked Pat who now appeared to be openly hostile to me.

"No, I never noticed it."

"I didn't drink too much last night. I'll take a trip round the island, in case she decided to go for a ride, and hit some trouble. Some of you can maybe take a walk around town to see if you can spot her."

"Thanks, Craig. I appreciate this," Rev. said.

"I'll meet you in the pub in about an hour. I'll need someone's mobile number so I can contact you and vice versa."

I exchanged numbers with Brent who was eager to let me see his huge phone that looked more like a small TV than a mobile phone.

I left them organising a search party - I noticed that some of the group weren't exactly rushing to volunteer.

I walked through the wind-propelled deluge back to my bike. I decided against going up to my room and putting on my leathers. The road would be quiet and it would take me twenty minutes at most to go around the coastline of the island. I retrieved my spare helmet from the luggage box and put it on.

I set off to navigate the island in a clockwise direction. When I had cleared the protection of the town's buildings the full force of the October gales assailed me. The bike suddenly became like a living animal and I had to balance speed against caution. It became a physical fight just to keep the machine upright and I was soon feeling the strain on every muscle. As I rounded the southern tip of the island, in some places the waves were being thrown up over the tarmac and I took care to ride on the wrong side of the deserted narrow road to minimise the chance of being washed away. If Deborah Grayson had tried to ride the bike with alcohol in her system, she may have fallen prey to the wrathful power of the sea.

I made slow progress up the western side of the island; I had to pause occasionally when the surge crashed the water high into the air and flooded the road.

There was no sign of either Grayson or her bike by the time I reached the ferry terminal. Not surprisingly, the service had been suspended due to the weather. As a result, I at least knew she was still on the island somewhere. I stopped at the terminal but neither Deborah Grayson nor her bike were in the car park. I checked my phone but there was no message from Brent or anyone else in the group.

I had almost completed a full circuit of the island when I reached the outskirts of the town - the eastern shore had offered nothing of note other than debris from the sea and broken tree branches that I had to navigate around.

There was one more possibility; a direct road between the terminal and the town that cut across the centre of the island. I turned on to Ferry Road and climbed up towards the crown of a small hill. I had travelled about four hundred metres into a small tunnel of trees when off to my right, I spotted a flash of crimson in the undergrowth. I slowed the bike, made a U-turn and scanned the trees to find the daub of red amongst the brown.

Deborah Grayson's bike was lying on its side in a patch of bracken and a short distance away was the woman herself. I didn't need to be a doctor to know that she was dead. Her arms and legs were angled in an unnatural position, like a rag doll that had been tossed to the ground by an angry child. As I approached I could see there was blood around her left temple and her eye socket had been fractured. She was wearing the same jacket and her legs were still covered in the black jeans she had worn the previous night. The storm had cast down twigs on her as if in haste to bury any trace of her. Her motorcycle helmet had been thrown or placed a few feet away. Despite the elaborate staging - which was designed to make it look like an accident - my gut instinct told me that Deborah Grayson had been murdered brutally.

A frisson of fear passed through me as I realised that I may have been one of the last people to see her alive. Pat McKean might jump to the wrong conclusion and I didn't like where that might lead.

Her wraithlike pallor and cyan-coloured lips told their own story. I leaned down and gently laid my hand on her neck to check her pulse; but it was merely a formality. Her sapphire eyes that once glittered were now dulled and still. I placed my fingers on her eyelids and gently closed them.

There was nothing else I could do for her other than to dial 999. When prompted by the woman, I asked for the police.

"Strathclyde police, what is your emergency?"

"I would like to report a murder."

The conversation that followed was filled with details of where I was, who the deceased was and where the body was located. There was some consternation as the officer at the other end of the phone realised that there was no chance of any detectives being dispatched to the island due to the weather. Even the force's helicopter was grounded.

"I'll pass you to CID in Largs."

I thanked the woman before some dull hold music occupied my ear for a minute or so. All around me the trees were creaking ominously as they were bent and rocked vigorously by the power of the storm.

"Largs CID, DS Mullen speaking," a gruff voice sounded over the cacophony.

"Detective Sergeant Mullen, my name is Craig Campbell and I would like to report a murder."

I repeated the details of the crime. He was skeptical and quizzed me as to why I thought it was a murder rather than an accident. The information that I was a private detective with some experience of murder scenes was not greeted with any enthusiasm by the irritated cop.

"You'll need to get a doctor to confirm the death, I'm sure there's one on the island," he said.

"Understood."

"Have you touched anything?"

"I tested for a pulse and closed her eyes but that's it."

"What are the conditions like at the location?"

"The body's in a small copse of trees lying on the leaf mulch, there are some bits of wood on top of her, blown there by the wind I think."

"There's a special constable on the island. I'll give him a bell and get him to come up to cover the body with a tarpaulin to try to preserve any evidence."

"I understand."

"We'll be there as soon as we can get on to the island. The forecast said the winds should ease enough in about six hours or so. We'll be there as soon we can get the chopper in the air."

"OK."

"And Mr Campbell, never mind trying any o' your private detecting," he warned.

"I wouldn't dream of it, DS Mullen."

As the rain began to fall once again, I called directory enquiries for the doctor's number. When it arrived on my phone, I called it immediately.

"Dr Endrick."

I relayed the facts to the doctor, who sounded thoroughly vexed that I had disturbed her on a Sunday morning. She told me she would be with me in about ten minutes and hung up the phone with ill-mannered abruptness.

I walked through the little wood to the side of the road to wave down the doctor when she arrived.

I called Brent.

"Craig, any news?"

"Is Neil with you?"

"Yes, he's here."

I could hear the phone being passed to Cairns. "Hi Craig."

"I'm sorry Neil but I've got bad news for you, Deborah's dead." There is no easy way to say that sentence. I kept it simple but I knew that it would shock and maybe even crush him.

"Oh dear God. Was it an accident?"

On an impulse I decided not to tell him the truth. "I think she came off her bike and hit a tree."

He asked a few questions about the circumstances and whom I had contacted. He sounded numb, remote from the conversation as if he was divorcing himself from his complicated emotions regarding his former partner. I completed the call and told him I would meet him and the rest of the group at the pub. He acknowledged me and ended the call.

Before the doctor could arrive, a beat-up old Ford Sierra pulled up just short of me driven by a young man. He stepped out of the car and dragged a heavy bundle of material from the passenger seat. When he stood up straight I could see he was around six feet six inches tall, rangy to the point of being gaunt. He looked anxious about the task that he faced.

"Hello, ah'm Greg Keddes, the special constable," he shouted in a broad Ayrshire accent above the noise of the wind that was screaming in the branches.

"Pleased to meet you Greg." I shook his hand.

"Did ye really find a boady?"

"She's over here."

As I began to lead him through the trees, a shining blue Mercedes pulled in behind the rusty derelict that was Greg's car.

"That's Doactor Endrick," the young man commented.

A sour-faced woman with a fleshy face and plump frame walked from the car and joined us. She thrust her hand towards me, "Campbell, I presume."

"Yes," I replied as she pumped my hand once with a degree of force that an army sergeant major would have been proud of.

"Keddes," she acknowledged my companion with a nod of her round head.

"Where is she?"

I pointed to where Debbie Grayson's life had been cut short.

The doctor strode purposefully off through the undergrowth to where the woman's body lay with the two of us trailing behind her. She reached the body, bent to check for life signs and said, "Yes, she's dead."

She then stood and was about to walk away. I put out a hand to stop her, "Do you think it was an accident?" I asked, hoping that she would confirm my suspicions of murder.

"That's for a pathologist and the police to establish. What's her name?"

"Deborah Grayson, her friends are in the town if you need any more details."

"No, that will be fine for now." She brushed passed me and walked back to the car.

I watched her go and was relieved that I wasn't subject to her idea of tender care.

I turned to see Greg turning a strange shade of pale green as he stared down at the broken form.

"You OK?"

"I..."

He swayed and before I could stop him, went down like he had been felled by a lumberjack's axe. He crumpled on top of Deborah's Grayson's corpse, lying across her to form a cross.

"Shit," I cried out.

With some difficulty I managed to get my hands under his armpits and roll him away from the woman. I hoisted his legs into the air and shouted his name. Slowly, he emerged from the faint and when he was fully conscious looked shame-faced.

"Ah'm sorry. Ah've never seen a deid boady afore."

"It's fine but you'll have to explain to the detectives when they arrive."

He looked forlorn. "They'll never let me intae the polis noo."

"I'm sure it'll be fine but you have to let them know what happened and give them a DNA sample. You'll not be the first cop that's fainted at the sight of their first corpse. So is that why you're a Special Constable, you want to join the police?"

"Aye, it's a good way tae get some experience when yir too young to sign up. The worst ah've hud tae deal wi' is aw the drunks oan a Saturday night and the odd break-in while ah waited for the real cops tae arrive."

"I'll take some photographs and then we'll need to cover her up to preserve the body and the crime scene as best as we can. Can you help?"

"Aye, ah think ah'll be awright noo."

I started to take some photographs, recording the scene before the weather destroyed anything that might be useful to the investigating officers. I looked around the nearby trees but there was no sign of the bike having collided with any of them. However, I did spot some blood on one Scots pine that looked like it was the cast off from someone striking Deborah repeatedly. I photographed it as it had already begun to be diluted by the rain.

I called the detective again and asked for an e-mail address. I told him about the blood spatter pattern on the tree and the lack of any damage that would have indicated an accident, which seemed to assuage some of his doubts about it being a murder. When the call was over I mailed him a copy of all the pictures I had taken.

The youthful future detective was standing with the tarpaulin and I helped him to open it. We covered the body and weighed down the cover with a combination of large branches and heavy stones.

When we were finished, Greg said, "The detective sergeant said ah wis tae stay here and secure the scene until they arrived. D'ye think ah'll be OK sitting in the moator?"

"I'm sure that'll be fine." At least he was getting some insight into the life he could expect as a uniformed cop.

I gave him my card and left him to his solitary vigil.

CHAPTER 4

I rode back into town, wondering which of the group would know that Deborah Grayson had been murdered. In a place like Millport the chance of a random killer was remote and I was sure that one of the Ducati club members had been pushed too far by Grayson's unpleasant personality and had reacted in the worst possible way.

It was a subdued and hushed assembly that greeted me when I walked into the pub. They were the only customers in the lounge but I could hear louder voices through in the public bar. Some of them sat nursing drinks, others were chatting in low voices. Everyone stopped and looked up when I arrived.

"Is it true?" Pat McKean asked.

"I'm afraid so."

I tried to read their faces, some were just shocked, and others like Colin Victor seemed to be almost relieved that she was gone. Neil Cairns was hard to read, his former calling meant that he was used to dealing with grief but maybe he still felt something for the woman that had betrayed him. The conflicting emotions continued to battle within him.

"Do you think she suffered?" Brent asked

"I don't think so," I lied.

"Sit down, we'll get you a drink,' Rhona McColl stood up and I asked for a soda water and lime.

Despite the warning from the officer in Largs, I couldn't help but wonder how I could probe gently to discover who killed Deborah Grayson. I had my own concerns that someone might point the finger of blame at me and if I could find the killer, I would avoid awkward questions when the police arrived. My previous visit to a jail cell was not one that I was keen to repeat.

I sat at a table with Pat McKean, Colin Victor and Neil Cairns.

"Did anyone see her after she left me last night?"

Pat was eager to talk, "I saw her with you outside but when I offered to walk her back to the flat she turned me down. She said she was going back to the pub for another drink."

"What about you Colin, were you still here?"

"Yes, I drank until closing time." He gave away nothing with his reply.

"Was she still here?"

"I don't know I didn't pay much attention to her."

I found that hard to believe as he had spent the earlier part of the evening glaring at her.

"Neil?"

"She was still here when I left. I had decided to leave about half an hour after she came back, I couldn't face her when she was so drunk." He paused as he had a different thought," I don't understand why she went out on the bike," he said with a bemused expression.

"Did she argue with anyone after I left?"

"She was pretty far gone and she was in a confrontational mood. I think there were words between her and Rhona after Debbie had a go at Brent again. She could be vicious sometimes and Rhona always seemed to want to antagonise her," Neil replied.

Rhona had delivered my drink and retreated back to the bar. I excused myself from the table and went to join her. She was dressed in a shapeless black top and a pair of unflattering grey trousers. She was deep in conversation with the barman, Nathan. I waited until he was called away to serve another customer before speaking to her.

"Neil said you and Deborah had a bit of an argument last night."

"Yes, what of it?"

"I was just wondering why she got under your skin so much. You seemed to be willing to argue with her at the drop of a hat."

"You saw her. She was an arrogant, self-centred bitch. She just got on my nerves."

"What was the argument about last night?"

"She'd had another go at Brent. He was angry but in truth he was hopelessly defenceless against her viper's tongue. He's just a daft big laddie with no real social skills but he didn't deserve the shit she was dealing out to him. She called him Shame Broon, slagged him off about asking her out and said the only reason he rode a bike was because his dick was so small. She was pissed and that just brought the most vile parts of her to the surface."

"How angry was he?"

"She humiliated him and you could see from his face that he was ready to lose it but I stepped in and stopped it getting any worse. I gave her a dressing down and then Nathan the barman stepped in. Told us to cool it or he would have to throw us out. He was furious, told her he'd had enough of her games and that if he threw her out she wouldn't get back in. I calmed down and she went into a sulk for a while but she was throwing herself at another guy within minutes."

I still wasn't convinced that her enmity towards Grayson was as simple as she said but there was little I could do to get to the bottom of it without letting them know that there was more to Grayson's death than they already knew.

I turned away from the bar to see Brent sitting glumly by himself. I decided I would get his take on the previous evening's events.

"Hi, Brent."

"Oh, hello."

"How are things?"

"I've been better."

"Rhona was saying you had another run in with Debbie last night."

"Yes."

"She insulted you."

"She always had to have a go at me."

"You must have been raging."

"I was livid. Did Rhona tell you some of the things she said?"

"Yes, she was definitely out of order. What started it? I thought you would have avoided her after her insults towards you earlier in the night."

"She was being really spiteful to Colin. He was at a different table but she was talking loudly about how she and her business partner had got Colin's company for a song because he was such a loser. Everybody was a loser according to her. It was only yesterday that she realised that he was the same guy she had put out of business and thought it was hilarious." He failed to keep the disgust she had provoked in him from appearing in his voice.

"Colin's not been in the committee very long has he?"

"No, why?"

"I was just thinking, it's strange that he wanted to be in contact with her if she had taken his business from him."

"I suppose so, I'd never thought about that.'

"Are you glad she's dead?"

He looked shocked. "No, why would you say that?"

"Well she did give you a hard time of it and from everything I've learned about her, it doesn't look like anyone will miss her."

"You're probably right. I could never understand why she had to behave the way she did. All I did was think she was attractive and ask her for a date. She turned on me and treated me like I was shit on the bottom of her shoe."

"When did you last see her?"

"I don't remember seeing her after the fight but I was pretty wrecked by then."

Colin Victor was on the move in the direction of the toilets and I decided to have a word with him over his connection with Grayson.

"I'll catch you later," I told Brent and followed Colin.

When we were standing at the wash-hand basins, I said, "You knew Deborah before you joined the club, didn't you?'

I thought he was a slightly pathetic figure in clothes that were ten years too old for him and wire-rimmed glasses that only aged him further. He looked through them at my reflection in the mirror above the sink with a level of rancour that he had been carrying for sometime. "What of it?"

"It seems a little strange that you would want to be in an organisation that she was in. Especially if she was responsible for you losing your business."

"I'm not allowed have a hobby?" he asked sarcastically.

"I'm not saying that but from my perspective it looks like you were stalking her."

"It's none of your business."

"Maybe not but the authorities are bound to ask questions about her death."

"Why it was an accident, wasn't it?"

"That's my opinion," I replied vaguely.

"Maybe the police will think differently. They've got more experience of judging these things. Maybe her bike was tampered with, maybe someone slipped something in her drink. I'm only saying it's a possibility," I suggested.

"I don't know what that would have to do with me, even if it's true."

"I think you have a pretty strong motive for wanting her dead and if I was a policeman, I'd be wondering why you decided to join the owner's club after she was involved in a business deal with you. A deal that you didn't come out too well on, from what I can gather."

He continued to rinse his hands like a demented Macbeth as he replied, "That bitch stole my company from me."

"How?"

"She owns some beauty shops and my company supplied them with quality soaps and hand creams. Out of the blue, the shops stopped paying their bills and we hit cash flow problems. We were close to administration when a finance company stepped in to make an offer. It wasn't great but I thought it would secure the jobs of the staff and I decided to accept it. She got my business for about a quarter of what it was really worth, and then let half the staff go and got her supplies for her shops dirt-cheap. It was all done through other people and it was only when I traced the company relationships that I discovered she was in fact a major shareholder in the firm that bought my business. It's a tactic she's used a few times on small suppliers, apparently. She didn't even know I had anything to do with it when I joined the club, I was just another face."

"Why join? What did you hope to achieve?"

"I wanted to find some dirt on her, something that I could take to the police or the tax man. Anything that would stop her from doing the same as she did to me to some other poor sap and costing more people their jobs."

"And that's it? You didn't fancy a more direct revenge?"

"What do you mean?"

"Murder."

"I'm not sorry the bitch is dead, I can't deny it but I didn't kill her or cause her accident if that's what you're saying."

"You would certainly have as a good a reason as anyone."

"So would half the people who knew her. What about Neil? She cost him his job, his marriage and then dumped him like last year's shoes. Last night he left the flat again after we got back from the pub."

"You were in a different place from Deborah?"

"Yes there were three of us in our flat. Brent, Neil and I."

"What time was this?"

"About twelve-thirty I think. He said he was feeling a bit rough after the wine he had had and wanted to clear his head."

"OK, thanks."

He moved to the drier and when he was gone I was left wondering about the former man of the cloth. Maybe the conflicting emotions he was exhibiting had more to do with guilt than regret or love. Grayson's constant flirting must have felt like sandpaper down his soul.

When I was finished, I walked out of the toilet with Neil Cairns in my sights.

"Fancy a walk, Neil?" I asked as I approached the table.

He looked up; his eyes were red and his face a ghastly grey. "I think I will. I could do with some air."

CHAPTER 5

We put on our jackets and set off towards the gardens of Garrison House, the civic centre of the island. The rain had stopped and the wind had eased a little but it was still difficult to walk against its strength.

"Tell me about Deborah," I said gently.

"I take it you know a little of our past?"

I nodded.

"When we met she was like no woman I had ever met. I had been with my wife since I met her at university. She's a good woman but - even for a Church of Scotland minister - it's difficult to hold a marriage together when the love has gone. She was comfortable with life just drifting on; we were more like housemates than man and wife. I had reached a point in my life where I was doubting both my commitment to my ministry and our relationship; a mid-life crisis I suppose you could call it. Deborah appeared when I was at my weakest, when I was most vulnerable to the flattering attention of an attractive younger woman."

"What happened?"

"I met her at a charity event and she turned on the full power of her charm, magnetism and sexuality. I felt like a teenager again, it was amazing. You understand what I mean, I watched her try all her tricks on you last night, but the difference was you were able to resist."

"I'm in a happy relationship with a woman I love. I'm not such an easy target," I said.

"You must think I'm stupid."

"It's not for me to judge; I wasn't in your shoes, facing your choices or doubts. What happened after that initial meeting?"

"She called me and invited me to another charity do. One of those posh, two grand a table events in Edinburgh. She made it clear that my seat was free as long as I didn't bring my wife. That's when the lies started and my fate was sealed."

"Why?"

"I told my wife I was going to a Church meeting and that I would be staying overnight. I told her there was a dinner with my colleagues, so she didn't think it was strange that I was packing a dinner suit. Deborah met me off the train in Edinburgh and she looked incredible. She had a way of dressing in a classy but very sexy way that stirred something in me that had been long dormant. She took me to the hotel and we made love for the first time before we even went to the dinner. I had never had an experience like it; she was tender but passionate, gentle but forceful. My wife was strictly a 'man on top, fifteen minutes maximum' kind of woman but it wasn't like that with Deborah." He appeared to be embarrassed by his confession and I felt a little sorry for him. He had been no match for a woman as sexually confident and manipulative as Grayson.

He continued talking as we entered the gardens where leaves and litter were swirling in little tornadoes. "After the dinner, we made love again for hours. I was both exhausted and exhilarated by the time I went down for breakfast. Our affair started there and for a month we would meet at her place and make love. Then I was foolish enough to ask her to go for a meal with me. One of my parishioners caught us holding hands in the restaurant and set off on a moral crusade to ruin me. He told my wife and the kirk elders and before I knew it I was getting divorced and had been asked to leave my church. If I'm being honest, I was so swept up in the romance - or maybe it was the lust - of my relationship with Deborah, that I didn't think about the harm I was doing to myself and others. I felt more alive than at any previous time in my life."

"How long did this last?"

"She began to lose interest in me not long after I signed the official separation papers. I lived with her for about five months but then she told me she had met someone else and threw me out. I was devastated; I couldn't believe that she had played me like some love-struck teenager. I couldn't handle it and I went to a dark place after that."

"Did you think of harming yourself?"

"Not quite but for a time I lost interest in life. I let myself go a bit, drinking too much, lying in bed half the day and stopped looking after my appearance. I grew my beard and changed my image. It was a pretty shitty time. I ended up going to see a psychiatrist."

"She had joined you in the owner's club when you were together?"

"That was another thing I loved about her. Unlike my wife, she used to delight in riding the bike with me and I spent a chunk of my savings to buy her a Ducati of her own. When we split up, I asked her not to come to the club but there was a nasty streak in her that enjoyed torturing people. It was an excuse to flaunt her affairs and to rub my failure in my face."

"That must have been very hard to take.'

"I admit there were times I hated her, like last night when she set her sights on you or the last time we were here it was Nathan, the barman. I couldn't understand why she felt it necessary to torment me. But there was another bit of me that still lusted after her and that feeling of unbridled joy she gave me. She was my addiction, I suppose."

"Did you ever tell her the effect that her behaviour was having on you?"

He turned to me and for the first time the true depth of his feelings became apparent. "It's impossible to make someone understand what you're feeling when they have no capacity for empathy. There were times I wanted to beat it into her."

"If it's any consolation, she told me last night that she did love you but then she got scared of her feelings." I said kindly.

"She had a funny way of showing it."

"So you're pleased she's gone?"

"I never said that. I have left those feelings of bitterness behind. I recently began a course in meditation with a Buddhist monk. He has taught me a lot about tolerance and conquering my dark thoughts."

His meditative control had not been too evident when he said he wanted to beat her. This was a man whose internal storms were as strong and possibly as dangerous as the current tempest enveloping the island.

"Colin said you went out again after you got back to the house. Is that correct?"

"Yes," he replied warily.

"Why?"

"One of the techniques I have learned is to find inner tranquility from all that nature has to offer. Even the wind and the rain can be useful to still your mind."

It sounded like a pile of crap but I let it slide. As we walked back towards the bar I asked some more questions about his life since the relationship with Deborah Grayson had ended. He told me even after his depression had ended he had become a bit of a recluse. Living alone in a rented flat, he had picked up some work in an organisation that helped train unemployed people to develop new skills. He said he had resolved himself to his new life and was feeling happy again until the news about Deborah had reached him.

It was very difficult to read how much of what he was telling me was real and how much was his attempt to deceive me or maybe even himself.

When we arrived back at the bar, Rhona was once again in deep conversation with Nathan who looked as if he was nodding politely in the right places but it was evident that his mind was elsewhere. Colin, Pat and Brent were congregated in a huddle around a table. Judging by the collection of glasses sitting in front of them, they had been knocking them back at some rate.

I draped my jacket over a chair and walked to the bar. Nathan excused himself from the conversation with Rhona, who went to join Neil.

"A pint of IPA, please."

As he began to pull the pint, I asked, "How well did you know Deborah Grayson?"

He looked up from his task. "Why do you ask?"

"Just making conversation. You mentioned that she thought she was fun, I thought maybe you knew a bit about her."

"I met her the last couple of times the club came over."

"She was an attractive woman."

"And?"

"I heard that she took a special interest in you the last time they visited."

"What if she did?" He handed me the pint aggressively and some of the beer sloshed over the sides.

"I was wondering if you had served her more than beer."

He took a hostile step towards me as if he was going to reach over the bar and grab me. I stood my ground and when he saw I wasn't going to back down he relaxed his stance.

"Look, I don't know who you think you are but it's none of your business."

"Did she leave with anyone last night?"

"How the hell should I know?"

"You're the barman. I imagined that you would notice these kind of things."

"Take your drink and let me be."

I paid him and sat beside Neil and Rhona.

"He's a bit tetchy."

Rhona looked a little guilty as she said, "That's probably my fault."

"Why?"

"Last night I told him about Debbie's little procedure."

"What?" Neil interjected.

"Oh shit." Rhona's face turned a brilliant shade of crimson.

"Deborah had an abortion about three months back," she continued softly.

"She didn't say anything to me. How did you find out?" Cairns asked.

"A friend of mine works at the clinic. She described this obnoxious patient they had and I thought she sounded a little familiar. My friend wouldn't tell me her name but she had only mentioned her because this patient had talked about motorbikes and my friend knew that I rode a Ducati. I challenged Deborah about it and she finally confessed that it was her. I'm ashamed to say I was gloating."

"Why would you gloat about something like that?" I asked, disturbed by her admission.

"The lifestyle she led, she thought there were never any consequences. Not that it mattered; to her it was probably like having an ingrown toenail removed," she said defensively.

"I'm sure it was as difficult a decision for Deborah as it was for any other woman, Rhona." Neil said.

"What's it got to do with Nathan?"

She hung her head. "He thinks he might be the father and Debbie had told him nothing about it."

"Shit. You're a class act, Rhona," I said as I grabbed my glass and walked through to the public bar before I said or did something I would regret.

Some of the islanders had gathered to watch the Sunday afternoon football on television. There was a low chatter of conversation and the atmosphere was lighter and more amiable than in the lounge.

I found a small table and sat down.

It appeared that there were any number of people who had a motive to see Deborah Grayson dead and now I had another suspect in Nathan. There had been coldness in the attractive woman that bordered on sociopathic behaviour and people who expected decency would find her conduct abhorrent. Did her lack of consideration cause Nathan to lose control and beat her to death? It was certainly a strong possibility.

Rhona McColl hadn't covered herself in glory either. Her actions were the least explicable; she had a hatred for Grayson than ran far too deep for it to be a simple case of female rivalry. I had to get to the bottom of her obsession with Grayson.

I looked around and noticed that Pat McKean was also in the bar watching the game. He seemed to be outside the group that had close contact with Grayson and he might be able to add some neutral commentary on those relationships.

I joined him and offered, "Can I get you a drink, Pat?"

He looked at me and considered his answer. I thought he was going to turn me down but then he said, "Aye, sure. A pint of Fosters."

When I returned with the drink, I asked him if it was OK to sit with him. He agreed but he still seemed reluctant. We spent the next twenty minutes watching the end of the first half of the game. Everton were beating Queen's Park Rangers by a single goal and the majority of the customers were watching it with distracted interest. Pat and I exchanged some thoughts about the merits of both sides and about football in general until the half-time whistle blew. Then

I saw an opportunity to quiz him about Grayson and the people she had upset.

"How well did you know Debbie?'

"Just through the club really. She wasn't someone I wanted to socialise with to be honest."

"Why do you say that?"

"She was a dangerous woman to become entangled with. She left a trail of destruction wherever she went."

"Like Neil?"

"And Colin, and Brent, and Rhona and God knows how many others."

"Rhona?"

"Yes, the most tragic of them all really."

"Why? What happened?"

"Rhona blamed Grayson for the death of her boyfriend and the loss of her baby."

"What?"

"It's a long story."

"I'm not going anywhere."

"It happened about two years ago. The guy's name was Ian Bryson. He was a member of the club, that's how the two of them met. He was a good guy, quiet but very passionate about the club and his bike. Rhona and him were living together when she became pregnant. Anyway, we had organised a weekend outing to Skye for the club members. We rode the bikes up and over to the island on the Friday. During the Sunday trip around the island, Debbie lost control of her bike and slid across the road at a sharp corner. She had fallen behind the majority of us and Ian had volunteered to stay with the slowest rider. He was the only one of the group who knew what had happened and stopped to help her. He had parked opposite the accident and was crossing the road when a car came round the bend. It was a blind corner; the poor driver couldn't do anything but hit him. He survived the initial impact but by the time the air ambulance got to him, it was too late. If he had still been wearing his helmet he would have been fine but he had left it on his bike. The docs reckoned it was a cerebral haemorrhage that killed him. Rhona had stayed at home because she was five months pregnant and didn't want to risk an accident. When the police arrived to tell her about Ian's death, she collapsed with the shock and it resulted in a miscarriage. Deborah Grayson didn't even come to Ian's funeral; she sent a note of apology about business commitments along with a wreath. Rhona never forgave her and despite the fact it was an accident, she was always convinced that Ian would still be alive if not for Debbie."

"Did she say anything to Grayson?"

"Not that I know of but you will have seen how they were with each other. Grayson was incapable of understanding other people's pain or even their resentment of her. She was so wrapped up in her own existence that nothing else mattered to her." I knew that she wasn't quite as indifferent as they all thought she was to their resentment.

"If everybody hated her so much, why put up with her in the club?"

"She kept volunteering to be treasurer and no one else could be bothered doing it. You know how it can be with an organisation like this; you get a role because you want it. Why are you asking all these questions?" he asked.

"Call it an occupational hazard; I suffer from terminal curiosity."

"I saw her kiss you last night."

It was my turn to feel defensive. "She tried to kiss me. She was hoping to change my mind about spending the night with her."

"And did she?"

"No, she was never my type."

"Is there more to Debbie's death than you've told us?"

"Maybe. Thanks for your help, Pat. I'll let you get back to the game." I shook his hand and walked back into the lounge before he could quiz me any more.

An idea of what had happened began to form but I had no way to prove my theory. Rhona's motive was very powerful and the staging of the accident was possibly the ultimate revenge for Ian's death. She had hoped that Debbie's murder would be dismissed as an accident, in the same way her lover's had been.

There was no sign of Rhona in the lounge and when I asked Brent where she had gone, he told me he thought that she had gone for a cigarette.

Outside, with the gale still blowing hard, I found Rhona huddled in the same shop doorway that I had been in with Deborah; she was trying to get some shelter from the wind but there was nowhere to avoid it completely. When she saw me coming she offered a pack of cigarettes.

"I don't smoke."

She put them away and then drew a large lungful of smoke from the one in her hand and in much the same way as

Debbie had done, blew it into the air above her where it was whisked away by the wind.

"I know about Ian," I said simply.

"And?" She was very prickly and suddenly on her guard.

"I've got reason to believe that Deborah Grayson was murdered."

"Is this where I'm supposed to break down and confess to killing the selfish bitch?"

"No, I just want to understand what happened last night. "

She studied me as she dragged on the cigarette again. "I'll weep no tears for her but I didn't kill her, although I've thought about it a lot in the past two years. She cost me everything."

"It was an accident."

"It was an avoidable accident; if she had just admitted that the bike was too much for her the accident might never have happened. We had all tried to warn her that the roads on Skye could be tricky but she insisted on going. She always liked to bag another conquest on our weekend rides and I don't mean a Munro. That was all it was about, she wanted to add another of the bikers to her list. I think her target that weekend was a young guy who had only joined the club and was on his first ride."

"There's no way that she meant for something to happen to Ian."

"I know that but it was her utter selfishness and contempt for anyone bar herself that caused it. Ian was a kind and considerate person, the type to ensure that everyone was safe. He took on the role of her protector on the road and it cost him his life," her voice cracked and for a short time I could see behind the hard image that she projected to protect herself from further pain.

"Why did you stay with the owner's club if she caused you so much hurt?"

"It was the connection to Ian, I suppose. Something we shared and loved that I didn't want to let go of."

"Do you know what happened last night?"

"I don't know for sure but after you left Nathan was trying to talk to Debbie. He was so angry about what I had told him."

"But that's what you hoped would happen isn't it? You had guessed that he might be the father."

She looked surprisingly remorseful as she said, "Yes. I hoped he would make her see what a selfish cow she really was. I wanted her to hurt in some way but in truth I'm not sure she was capable of it. There was a profound coldness about her that I have never seen in anyone else. She seemed to be devoid of empathy, never mind empathy she couldn't even manage sympathy. It was like other people didn't exist except as a means to her pleasure or profit."

"What did you think Nathan was going to do?"

"I don't know. I didn't want him to kill her."

"So you think he did?"

She took her time in answering before she said, "I think it's possible. He was angry enough and he used to be a soldier, so he had the temperament and the skills, I suppose."

"I doubt that you would ever be convicted of anything but it seems to me that you loaded the gun and pointed it in the right direction. If he did kill her, you'll have to live with that for the rest of your life. I don't envy you."

I walked out of the shop doorway and left her to her cigarettes and regrets.

What could I do about Nathan? If he had killed Grayson, he was equally capable of killing me. I would have to confront him but it would need to be with some form of guarantees for my own safety.

Back at the pub, I ordered a coke and stood at the bar. When there were no other customers nearby, with my heart hammering in my chest, I leaned over and said, "We need to talk."

He looked at me with caution laced with steel. "What about?"

"Deborah Grayson."

"What about her?"

"It would be better if we talk in private. Is there somewhere we could go?"

"There's a flat upstairs but I don't see what it has to do with you."

"Let's say I know that you and she had more in common than just having a laugh."

He growled to the barmaid, "Becky, keep an eye on the place would you?"

"OK, will you be long?" the older woman replied.

"No." He gestured with his head indicating that I should follow him.

"Neil, I'm going for a chat with Nathan." It was the only small measure of protection I could buy myself.

For his part, Neil gave a bemused look and said, "Fine."

I followed the landlord up a narrow staircase that he seemed to fill and loom over me. He led me into an unpretentious but stylish living room.

"Get on with it, whatever it is you've got to say," he said standing at the window that was rattling with the strength of the wind.

"I know about the baby. I know you were upset when Rhona told you and I know that you needed to talk to Debbie. Now she's lying dead in a wood."

"And you think I killed her."

"Yes."

"Well you're wrong."

"Convince me," I said with more assurance than I felt.

"Do you have kids?" he asked.

"No."

"Neither do I. I was married for ten years. We tried everything to have a baby but nothing happened. The doctors couldn't find anything wrong with either of us but it tore us apart. It was probably the thing that caused us to get divorced, the gut-wrenching grief for the death of something that never was."

"I had come to the island to get away from everything; the army; my ex-wife; even my family who always wondered why I hadn't become a father. It was to be a new start and the dreams of fatherhood were left behind in my old life."

"I met Deborah a year ago when the club came to the bar. She was vivacious and fun loving, we had a few laughs and I slept with her. No attachments, no complications. When she came back earlier in the year it was the same thing, great sex with no strings, at least that's what I thought."

"And then Rhona changed all that last night when she told you what had happened," I prompted.

"I should have know something was wrong when Deborah walked in. There was a distance between us. When I saw her flirting with you, I thought she had just moved on to someone new, no skin off my nose."

"I couldn't believe it when Rhona told me about the abortion. It was like Debbie had ripped out my heart and tramped all over it. I would have done anything for that kid. She wouldn't even have needed to be involved if she hadn't wanted to. He or she could have come and lived on the island with me. It would have been a good life for a kiddie."

"So you spoke to Debbie?"

"Eventually I persuaded her to talk to me. I brought her up here but she sat there and told me that it had nothing to do with me. At first she denied it was mine and when I tried to get her to tell me whose baby it was, she finally confessed that I was the father. I asked her why she didn't tell me and do you know what she said?" he asked.

I shook my head.

"She said that it was her body and that she couldn't have carried a child to full term, she didn't want stretch marks. Fucking stretch marks, can you believe that?" Instead of the fury that I had expected he seemed to become overwhelmed by grief. Tears formed in the corner of his eyes.

"I've never despised anyone more than I despised her at that moment but honest, I never killed her. I told her to get out of my sight but by the time I got back down to the bar she was laughing and joking as if nothing had happened. It was then that I realised that she was incapable of giving a damn about anyone or anything other than herself. How are you supposed to relate to someone like that?"

"I don't know, Nathan. I don't know. Did you see anyone following Debbie when she left?"

"No but as I was closing up, Eileen Jackson, one of the locals came looking for her. She had been trying to talk to her earlier in the night but Debbie had avoided her, like she had avoided me."

"What did she want to talk about?"

"I don't know but Eileen was pretty pissed about whatever it was."

"OK, thanks. I'm sorry for what you've been through."

"Me too; sorry I ever met the cold-hearted bitch."

I walked back down into the pub with my mind full of confusion. What was Eileen Jackson's connection to the dead woman?

CHAPTER 6

I gathered my jacket from the lounge bar, letting everyone know that I was going back to my guesthouse and that I would be back later.

The wind seemed to have strengthened once again and I found it nearly impossible to walk upright as the strongest gusts buffeted me. As I struggled towards the guesthouse, I had no idea what motive Jackson may have had to commit murder. Could it be jealousy or was she another victim of Grayson's unethical business practices? Maybe I had misread what had happened to Deborah and that she was truly an unfortunate casualty of an alcohol-fuelled accident and Jackson had nothing to do with her death.

I arrived at the house and walked towards the small lounge that was attached to the kitchen. Eileen Jackson was sitting in a large armchair with a notebook computer on her lap. She looked up at me as I entered, her emerald eyes peering over the top of a thin pair of spectacles. At her side there was a substantial ashtray where smoke curled as it rose from a hand-rolled cigarette; the smell of something other than tobacco and the slight disconnected look that she wore told me exactly what it was.

"Mr Campbell, what can I do for you?"

"We need to have a little chat about Deborah Grayson?"

There was a brief pause before she said, "Who?"

"Don't give me that crap. You went looking for her last night at the bar."

"So?" The relaxed air she had held disappeared and she was suddenly on edge, alert and coiled.

"I would like to know why you were so desperate to see her."

"It's none of your business."

"Maybe not but it'll certainly be of interest to the police."

"What are you talking about?"

"I've got witnesses who say that you were the last to see her. That the two of you were in a heated argument about something." I was winging it but my instincts told me I was on the right track.

The first traces of panic appeared and she seemed to age as I studied her. "They're lying, I never found her." The marijuana she had smoked had loosened any control she had over her body language and it was obvious to me that she was spinning me a lie.

"That's not true. As I said, I have witnesses. If I look harder I might even be able to find someone who saw her in your car." I was telling my own story with more conviction than she had conjured when she told hers.

Her control had gone completely and she screamed, "I don't know what you're talking about, they couldn't have seen her, she was in the boot."

My gamble had paid off and she was suddenly quiet.

"You killed her but I'm not sure why. It'll be easier for you if you admit what happened; I know how difficult she was. I'll even help you with the police if I can."

She stood up, her face now contorted into an ugly vision of scorn. The rage she was feeling only increased her sense of abandon and she looked completely different. Antagonism, bitterness and resentment spilled out of her.

"You met her?" she spat the question like a cornered animal.

"Of course."

"She was a premier class cow. She deserved to die."

"Why would you say that? What had she done to you?"

"Do you know why she wanted to come to Millport every year?"

"I thought it was a committee decision."

"Ha. She just had to bat her eyelashes and flash her tits and the men in that club would have jumped off a cliff if she told them to."

"So why did she want to come here?"

"Because I was supplying her with some first-rate pot for her to sell on the mainland. Her whole business was built on the proceeds of drug money and then she used those same businesses to launder the money she was making from what I was supplying her."

"This whole thing is about drugs?" I asked in surprise. I had thought her earlier hints about being able to give me something to help me relax would have come from her own personal store. I hadn't even considered her being a dealer or a supplier.

"Finally, the penny drops."

"How did this operation work?"

"The great thing about living on an island is that it gives you a great excuse to own a boat. Four times a year I sail around to the west coast of Arran and meet a ship that comes in from Holland. They deliver a package and I bring it back here. She would come over and pick it up, then go back to the mainland to sell it."

"Sounds like a profitable little enterprise."

"It was until that bitch got too greedy. She told me the last time she was here that she needed more product. I told her I didn't want to get any more because I didn't want the police or the customs people to catch on to what we were doing."

"And?"

"I knew there was something wrong when she kept avoiding me in the bar. I had to speak to her to see what the problem was, that's why I went back when the pub was closing. She was walking back to her flat when I caught up with her. She was drunk, we fought, and she fell and struck her head. It was an accident, that's all it was. I got the car and drove her up to the wood and dumped her."

I knew she was lying as I had seen the evidence of Grayson being struck more than once in that very wood. It was a tale designed to deceive and get her a lesser sentence but there was no substance to it at all. "So why not phone for an ambulance?" I asked.

"I was frightened. I didn't want them to find out about the drugs."

"It's an interesting story but I know it's not the truth. Do you want to try again?"

She suddenly grabbed the ashtray and swung it at my head. I saw it late but managed to avoid the worst of the force, although it did catch me a glancing blow high on the temple. The power drained from my legs and I collapsed to the floor. As the room spun around me, I watched her run out the door.

CHAPTER 7

It took a couple of minutes before the dizziness cleared enough for me to stand up. When I did a wave of nausea hit me and I took a few huge gulps of air before I could stagger out into the street.

I turned towards the sea and moved as quickly I could with my head pounding. The streets were deserted as people stayed sensibly indoors out of the reach of the storm. When I reached the shore side road I looked left and right. I spotted her climbing down a ladder at the side of the old pier towards a small boat. Surely she couldn't be thinking of trying to sail in this weather.

"Eileen, stop," I screamed into the howl of the wind and the sea.

Either she couldn't hear me or chose to ignore me. Between the blow to my head and the rage of the tempest, I struggled to move with any speed. I could only watch as she dropped into the small craft and cast off from the pier. Even in the shelter of the bay, the boat was being tossed like a cork in the squall.

"Eileen don't, you'll kill yourself," I shouted uselessly.

Her target was a yacht that was at anchor about two hundred metres from the pier. Her course was erratic but she finally managed to get close to the larger vessel. As she reached for the rope that would allow her to secure the dinghy, an enormous wave crashed into the yacht and carried her into the sea. Numb, I stood for ten minutes and looked out into the bay but she never resurfaced.

I made a call to the emergency services but knew that that there was little that could be done. The man on the end of the phone told me that a lifeboat would be dispatched as soon as possible. I gave him my number and told him where he could find me.

When the call was complete, I flopped down on a nearby bench and tried to regain some composure. Her story made no sense, there was no way she could have manhandled Grayson into a car and then dump her in the woods. How did she get the bike there? She must have had some help from someone. There had been no sign of her spouse at the guesthouse, so who could it have been?

I crossed back to the relative shelter of the buildings and made my way to the bar. As I walked I did my best to clear my head and an idea occurred to me that might just make the accomplice expose him or herself. I wouldn't tell them what had happened to Jackson at this point and try to use her to bring out the other killer.

The committee members were collected together around a group of three tables, much like they were when I first met them.

"Nathan, any chance of a cup of coffee?" I asked as I reached the bar, hoping that I didn't look too disorientated.

He agreed and said he would bring it to the table. I chose a chair at the end of the group of tables and sat down.

"Any news about the ferry yet?" Colin asked

"No, nothing. The storm's still pretty bad."

"You think Debbie was murdered don't you?" Brent asked out of the blue.

"Yes, I do and I think my landlady might know who the killer is. She was looking for Debbie late last night and maybe she saw what happened. I went to speak to her but she was out visiting friends. I called her and she said she should be home soon. I'm going to go round in half an hour to hear what she has to say."

"Could it be another local? Someone your landlady knows," Colin Victor suggested

"I don't know."

The conversation drifted away and people sat contemplating their drinks. I tried to read how they were behaving, as I was sure one of them had helped to kill Deborah Grayson. No one gave anything away and I had to hope that my second gamble of the day would pay off.

After ten minutes, I finished my coffee and went through to the public bar. I told them I was going to watch the second football match of the day to take my mind off the murder.

I had already noticed that the public bar had a door out to a beer garden at the back of the pub. In the little patio there was a gate that led to a narrow close that took me back out on to the seashore road. I hurried through the latest gusty shower that was passing over the island. I glanced at the bay but there was no sign of the RNLI lifeboat.

Back at the guesthouse, I sat in the chair that Eileen Jackson had been sitting in just an hour earlier.

I didn't have to wait long before I heard the latch on the outside door. The pain in my head was increasing and I was scared that I would pass out before I could secure the killer.

"Eileen," a man's voice shouted. I recognised it and immediately I knew who had helped to kill Debbie Grayson.

"What the hell are you…" The man said as he opened the door.

"Neil, I was really hoping it wouldn't be you," I said sadly.

He made no attempt to deny it, no bluster or anger. He revealed a feeling of contrition and resignation as he sank into the other armchair.

"Where is she?" he asked.

"In all likelihood, dead. She tried to escape on her yacht but a wave caught her as she was boarding and swept her into the water. I doubt she could survive in those conditions."

"Stupid woman," he responded sadly.

"Do you want to tell me what happened?"

"Does it matter?"

"Yes, it does. I need to understand"

He sighed and slow tears meandered down his ashen face. "You know what Deborah was like, you saw her in action. There was a lot I learned about her after she left me that made me think she had done me a favour when she left but there was still that piece of me that held on to some hope that we would get back together. It was an idiotic thing to believe but it was the root of a jealousy I just couldn't shake."

"Last night when I saw her throwing herself at you it made me so angry. When I got back to the flat I was still boiling and I didn't feel like going to sleep. I thought a meditative walk would help but I came across Eileen searching the streets.

She was looking for Debbie and obviously knew about our relationship. She asked me if I knew where Deborah was. I told her I didn't but I would help her to find her."

"We walked about the town for about twenty minutes before we found her. Debbie was sitting down near the pier, close to the old terminal building smoking a joint. When she saw us she just laughed. Eileen was already furious and the look on Debbie's face made my feelings of betrayal resurface. She said that the two of us made an ideal couple, old and decrepit, like we were some comedy duo. She then went on about how we'd be the only couple whose bones would creak more than the bed when we were… the word she used was fucking. It was disgusting the way she behaved."

"When she had finished laughing at the thought of Eileen and I together, she told Eileen that she had found a new supplier and that Eileen would have to find a new pension scheme. Eileen slapped her but it made no difference, Debbie just shouted that we were a pair of losers. A failed minister and a failed drug dealer." He fell into a contemplative silence.

"What happened Neil?" I prompted.

"She was so insulting, so dismissive that I just couldn't take it any more. I reached down and picked up a rock, swung at her head and she collapsed. All the fury I was feeling just disappeared, and I started to panic. Eileen said that we should throw her in the sea but I just couldn't do that. I suggested we make it look like a bike accident. Eileen was reluctant but I managed to persuade her. While she went for her car, I stood over Debbie's body, worried that someone would discover us. Fortunately or as it turned out unfortunately there was no one around and when Eileen arrived back we loaded her body into the boot. Eileen drove me round to the house that Debbie was staying in to get her bike. Debbie had the keys in her bag, so I got on the bike and I followed Eileen up to the woods." There was another long silence.

"She wasn't dead though was she?" I suggested.

"No. We were laying her out, trying to make it look like an accident; I thought it would be dismissed as a result of her drinking. Before we finished staging the scene, Debbie suddenly groaned. Before I could react, Eileen just beat her twice with another rock until Debbie was silent; there was nothing I could have done to stop her. I was so shocked I was paralysed, I couldn't think what to do next. Eileen took charge, she told me that no one must know what had occurred and as long as we stuck to our stories no one would ever find out that we had killed her. She told me she couldn't go to jail and that we had to stick to the story. That's why I was so surprised when you told us that she was going to give you the details. I thought that she was going to spin some story to make it look as if I was the only killer."

"She had told me a different version that didn't mention you at all."

"Oh."

"But I knew it was a lie; I knew that she needed help to get Debbie's body to the woods. Did you know about the drugs thing?"

He shook his head. "No, not before last night."

Although I was disappointed that he was involved, I was also incensed at how calculating he had been all day. "That was quite an act this morning. Maybe the prison will have a drama club," I said sarcastically.

"I just blanked it from my mind, as if it had never happened. Right up until you mentioned Eileen and then it all came rushing back."

"The police will be here when the storm eases. You need to tell them all you've told me."

"I know. Don't worry, if anyone knows the importance of repentance now, it's me."

EPILOGUE

Four hours later the storm had abated enough to allow the police helicopter to deliver two detectives and a scene of crime officer to the island. I had persuaded Nathan to allow Neil Cairns and I to occupy his flat until the police arrived.

Detective Chief Inspector Urquhart was the senior investigating officer and he was less than impressed by my interference, despite me presenting him with all the answers in a neat bundle.

"I should do you with perverting the course of justice, son," he growled.

"But you won't. You're welcome to take all the credit with the press. I'll not tell them if you don't."

"You're a chancer, Campbell."

"It's a living."

His sour face told me that he wasn't blessed with much of a sense of humour. "Go downstairs and give your statement to DS Mullen." He walked away to speak to Neil Cairns who was now both a physical and emotional wreck.

There was a bit of me felt a little sympathetic towards a man whose life had been ruined twice by the same woman. She had manipulated, tormented and betrayed him. A woman who was not worthy of him had cost him his calling, his wife and now his freedom.

When I walked back into the lounge, Nathan said, "They found Eileen's body."

I acknowledged him with a brief nod, it was another pointless death.

I gave my statement to DS Mullen, who was even less impressed with my efforts than his boss had been after the warning he had given me. I let his disdain wash over me; I was desperate to get off the island as soon as possible and end my 'relaxing' weekend. I did commend the young special constable to the detective in the hope that his diligence would help his career dreams to come true.

By the time I escaped the Mullen's clutches it was too late to board a ferry and I was trapped for another night. I lay on the bed and finished my book.

My phone rang and I could see from the display that it was Carol. "Hi darling, that's me back. Where are you?" she asked.

"Still in Millport. The ferry was off due to the weather. How was your weekend?"

"We maybe drank a bit too much but it was great. You?'

"Oh, very quiet."

THE END

ABOUT THE AUTHOR

Sinclair Macleod was born and raised in Glasgow. He worked in the railway industry for 23 years, the majority of which were in IT.

A lifelong love of mystery novels, including the classic American detectives of Hammett, Chandler and Ross Macdonald, inspired him to write his first novel, The Reluctant Detective. It was followed by 'The Good Girl' and 'The Killer Performer" also featuring Craig Campbell.

He has also written a series of police procedural novels set in Glasgow featuring Detective Superintendent Tom Russell and Detective Inspector Alex Menzies. 'Soulseeker', Inheritance', 'The Harlequin' and 'Grave Consequences' are also available from Marplesi Books.

Sinclair lives in Bishopbriggs, just outside his native city with his wife, Kim and daughter, Kirsten.

47905CB00009B/3202